The Brechin Tales

Terry Isaac

with Iris Thornhill

Hamish McMoosie's Christmas Present

Illustrated by Mandi Madden

ISBN 1873 891 652

Published by Brechin Tales Shop Ltd
P.O. Box 665, Brechin, Angus, Scotland DD9 6JS
Tel/Fax: 01356 624648
Email: **brechinhouse@hotmail.com**

Printed by Wm Culross & Son Ltd, Coupar Angus
Tel: 01828 627266   Fax: 01828 627146

The Brechin Tales

Hamish McMoosie's Christmas Present

Dedication

Dedicated to the memory of

Ian Sommerville of D C Thomson

Who was the inspiration for this tale

```
Isaac, Terry

Hamish
McMoosie's
Christmas
                    JF

1494152
```

Thank you for buying another in the series of

The Brechin Tales

Hamish McMoosie's Christmas Present

Hamish McMoosie's Christmas Present

In the Old City, the first snows of December had arrived in flurries and scurries, blown by the North Wind on its journey South to Edinburgh and beyond. The earth slumbered beneath its thick white winter overcoat and the rooftops of the old stone buildings wore crisp tam-o'-shanters of snow.

The old house near the cathedral grounds had seen three centuries of winters and another winter would just add a few more scars to its weathered stone. The ancient frosted stone walls stood bold against the bitter wind. If you had very good eyes and looked very closely, you might just notice that the snow had melted a little around a tiny window, in a tiny cottage with a tiny door hidden beneath the worn stone steps of the old house. The

tiny cottage was the home of Hamish McMoosie and his wife Dorma.

Inside the cosy cottage, warmed in the coral glow of a peat fire, Hamish McMoosie's paw

traced patterns on the frosted glass of the window and

smiled a little contented Hamish smile. Christmas

would soon be here, just seven frosted days and

eight twinkling moonlit nights to go.

All over the Old City mice children had been

ticking off the days until Christmas on their

Advent calendars and their long pink noses

had made little circles of mist on the glass

of the Toy Shop window as they pressed

their faces to it to peer in and see all the wonderful Christmas toys displayed there. The

mouse-children dreamed of finding their empty Christmas stockings, which they would

hang from the fireplaces on Christmas Eve, being found chubby and bulging with gaily-

wrapped surprises when they awoke on Christmas morning.

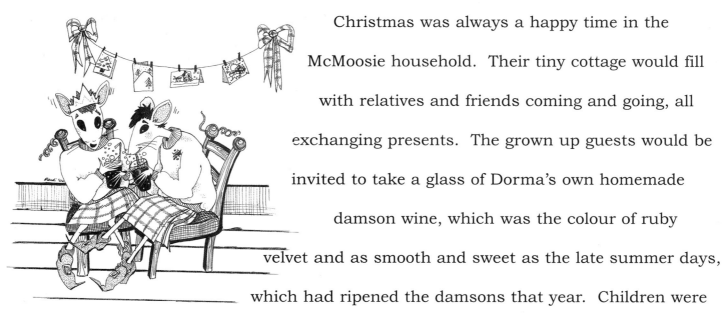

Christmas was always a happy time in the McMoosie household. Their tiny cottage would fill with relatives and friends coming and going, all exchanging presents. The grown up guests would be invited to take a glass of Dorma's own homemade damson wine, which was the colour of ruby velvet and as smooth and sweet as the late summer days, which had ripened the damsons that year. Children were served a sweet dark brew with fizzy bubbles that giggled up their noses.

By September Dorma had all her spice-perfumed Christmas puddings made, and by October rich fruitcakes lay maturing, snuggled together in dark tins, waiting to be woken to wear their festive coats of marzipan and icing. By November the marble shelf in the larder almost groaned under the extra weight of Christmas food – game pies with rich savoury jelly holding the meats inside the crisp crusty pastry, and, of course (for this was a mouse household) a whole harvest of different coloured cheeses were stacked nearby, from the palest yellow to a deep orange, promising wonderful Christmas eating.

Dorma had her Christmas List pinned up on the notice board that she had got Hamish to put up on one of the walls in the gaily-painted kitchen. Hamish was not very good at doing odd jobs around the home and he had never quite got the notice board to hang straight, so for the past eleven years it had hung at a peculiar angle. From time to time, Hamish promised to unscrew the notice board and put it back correctly but Dorma said that it was now a feature of the kitchen and best left as it was. The truth was that Dorma could not be sure that Hamish would ever put it back correctly. Hamish had the habit of starting jobs and never finishing them, and Dorma felt that even a wonky notice board

was better than no notice board at all.

Dorma was standing looking at her list, sipping a steaming cup of rosehip tea and she hummed as she read down her list and crossed out the items one by one. "Yes", she told herself, "all is progressing nicely. Just a few things left on the list – those that Hamish has to do!" Much as Dorma would have liked Hamish to have completed all of his jobs by now, she was taking things slowly, as she did not want to cause arguments. Dorma needed Hamish to be in a good mood as she had something to tell him. In fact, she had several things to tell Hamish, and she was just waiting for the right moment to tell him. One of the things she needed to tell Hamish was that Dorma's Great Aunt Maude would be staying with them over Christmas.

Aunt Maude and Hamish did not get on well. Aunt Maude thought Hamish a complete waste of space but then, Aunt Maude thought most husbands a complete waste of space!

Aunt Maude had had five husbands herself – two she had outlived and of the other three – one had run away to join the Navy and the remaining two had just run away. Aunt Maude always carried a black umbrella with a carved goose-head handle and a sharp point on the end. She had the habit of poking the pointed end into Hamish's rear whenever he annoyed her, which unfortunately for Hamish was quite often. 'Yes', thought Dorma, 'I will have to choose the right moment to tell Hamish about Aunt Maude'.

Back in the sitting room, Hamish continued to trace patterns on the window. The sweet-smelling Christmas pine tree, which he had cut down from the forest, was still propped up outside the front door waiting for Hamish to plant it in its bright red Christmas pot. The box of tree decorations was still in the loft, awaiting Hamish to bring them down and the shimmering tinsel Christmas garlands and bright paper lanterns were still in a corner, where he had dumped them days ago.

Hamish was thinking about Christmas Eve when, playing his beloved bagpipes, he would lead the mouse congregation in the candlelit Carol Service in the cathedral. Hamish McMoosie may have had many faults, but the one thing no one could criticise was his playing the bagpipes. When Hamish took up his pipes and blew into the chanters, the very earth would stop to listen. It was the

most beautiful of sounds.

On a warm waft of spice and other Christmassy smells Dorma's voice drifted in from the kitchen. "Hamish, dear, if you have a spare moment, would it be too much trouble to set the Christmas tree in its pot and bring it in. And this year, Hamish, I would like you to decorate it".

"Decorate the Christmas Tree?" whispered Hamish to himself, "Dorma always decorates the tree!" But then, he mused, Dorma had been doing some very odd things just lately. For instance Dorma had been secretly knitting six fluffy, pale yellow, Angora wool covers for his golf clubs. Hamish knew they must be a surprise Christmas present for him because every time he came in the room, Dorma tidied her knitting away behind a cushion. Hamish had pretended not to see, so as not to spoil the surprise, and did not want to hurt Dorma's feelings, but really he wished she had asked him what he wanted.

He had tried the six fluffy covers on the heads of his woods in

his golf bag when Dorma was not looking and they did fit OK.

But really... fluffy Angora wool, and pale yellow! He thought the

other mice at the golf club would think him a sissy! And why, thought

Hamish, had Dorma filled their linen cupboard with all those

little white towels? There must be three dozen of them, and

they were hardly big enough to cover his face, let alone his

body, after a shower.

Two more days went by before Dorma mentioned the tree and

decorations again, and this time she added that she was preparing

Hamish's favourite supper – haggis, mashed neeps and tatties – and she

wouldn't want it to get cold waiting for the tree to be potted. The thought of

Dorma's wonderful cooking was enough to spur Hamish into action and get him out of his comfortable armchair in the best spot near the fire.

Hamish put on his bright yellow anorak, found his fleece-lined Wellington boots and put them on, snuggled a warm tartan muffler around his neck, and creaked open the big front door to step out into the crisp, chill air. Within an hour he had finished potting the Christmas tree, dragged the sweet smelling forest fir into the sitting room, and even found time to get the decorations out of the loft before supper.

Dorma made the most wonderful haggis suppers; her mashed turnip was rich with butter and black pepper, and her creamed potatoes light, white and fluffy as the snow outside.

Because it was nearly Christmas Dorma had placed a sprig of holly in the centre of the steaming haggis, which was given pride of place on a large blue-patterned plate set in the centre of the gay Gingham cloth, which covered the table. Dorma lit the two large candles

she had placed at either end of the haggis and turned out the kitchen lights. She took off

her apron, folded it neatly and joined Hamish at the table.

 "A meal fit for a King", squeaked Hamish and a wide contented smile moved across his

face. "Can there be anything more romantic than haggis by candlelight?" added Hamish.

Dorma smiled.

When Hamish had nearly finished his supper,

and seemed to Dorma, to be in a very good

post-haggis mood; Dorma thought she

would tell him some of her news.

"Hamish, dear," she began, sweetly,

"Aunt Maude will be coming to spend

Christmas with us – she is arriving on Christmas

Eve." There was a pause, then a gulp, then a rasping, coughing sound as Hamish choked

on his last bite of haggis.

"Aunt Maude, Dorma! Aunt Maude? Aunt Maude at Christmas!!" choked out Hamish

through a splutter of haggis.

"My dear", said Dorma, "It is the season of goodwill to all, and this year

I need her help".

"Well you are not showing much goodwill to me

inviting that female dragon here at Christmas",

complained Hamish.

Dorma began to cry. A big soft wet tear gently rolled

down her cheek, followed by another one and yet

another. Hamish was really quite a kind-hearted

mouse and never could stand Dorma's tears. He sighed a big sigh and put his arm around Dorma's shoulders. Unbeknown to Hamish, Dorma also had another piece of news for him but as he had acted so strongly about Aunt Maude, she thought she had better keep it for another day.

Christmas Eve came too soon for Hamish. He was sitting in his favourite armchair when Dorma called out, "Hamish, have you decorated the tree yet? Have you hung the decorations? Aunt Maude will be here in an hour!" Of course, Hamish had not, and the decorations were still lying exactly where he had put them days earlier.

The thought of Aunt Maude's imminent arrival - and particularly the thought of the sharp pointed end of her umbrella - spurred Hamish into action as never before. In what seemed like a twinkling of an eye, the bare tree in its red tub was dressed in a magnificent, shimmering ball-gown of twinkling diamond lights, tinsel garlands, and gay baubles of every shape and hue. A magical fairy holding aloft a sparkling wand was positioned at the top.   Brightly coloured Chinese paper lanterns and paper chains of red, green and silver hung from the four corners of the sitting room. In fact, though Hamish thought so himself, he had done a very good job - and only just in time!

The impatient jangling of the front doorbell echoed loudly through the little cottage. It seemed to Hamish that the walls trembled slightly when the sharp tap of a metal-tipped umbrella followed the ringing on the doorbell. Aunt Maude had arrived. "Hamish, would you let Aunt Maude in please?" said Dorma's voice from the kitchen.

Hamish, his whiskers drooping, walked slowly along the hall and drew back the bolt of the

big, old, oak front door. It seemed reluctant to open. The old hinges groaned and creaked

a protest and the door dragged squealing along the floor before opening wide enough to

allow Aunt Maude to enter. A chill blast of air entered the little cottage as Aunt Maude

flounced past Hamish on her way to the kitchen, as if Hamish

was merely the doorman.

Hamish closed the door and joined Aunt Maude and Dorma.

"All ready for the big event I hope Hamish?" enquired Aunt

Maude.

On getting no immediate answer, Aunt Maude peered over the top

of her bifocals and fixed Hamish with a stare, "Hamish, today is the

twenty fourth of December. What is supposed to happen

tomorrow?"

Well, any fool knows that Christmas Day happens on the 25th of December thought Hamish, but if Aunt Maude decided otherwise then the whole world might discover that Christmas day was in fact the thirty first of March. Aunt Maude was that sort of person. Hamish was about to stutter the obvious reply when Aunt Maude added, "Come on, Hamish! Answer! Cat got your tongue? What is happening tomorrow? It's not that difficult is it?" Without giving Hamish a chance to reply, Aunt Maude looked down at him and shook her head in disbelief. Hamish, meanwhile, looked carefully at Aunt Maude's right paw, holding the long black umbrella with the goose-head handle, just in case it began to move in his direction.

"Really Hamish, answer the question! Are you a man or mouse?" continued Aunt Maude. Now Hamish knew a trick question when he heard one, and he knew whichever answer he came up with was likely to be wrong. He was very relieved when Dorma placed a large glass of damson wine into Aunt Maude's paw, and hastily changed the subject; "How pretty you look in your tartan skirt, Aunt Maude, is it new?"

"Erumpth, husbands!" snapped Aunt Maude, ignoring Dorma's compliment, "nothing but blether!" Aunt Maude flounced out of the kitchen without a backward glance, and Hamish was almost sure that the goose-head handle sneered at him as Aunt Maude swept down the hall to

the sitting room like some great ocean liner at full speed.

When Hamish followed her into the sitting room he found Aunt Maude had plonked herself down on his favourite chair. With a very stern voice she, and when she suggested

that she and he should really have a talk. Hamish remembered all the jobs he could be doing which would take him as far away from Aunt Maude as possible and hurried left..

 Hamish managed to keep some distance between him and Aunt Maude until the evening. In spite of Aunt Maude's presence Hamish was looking forward to Christmas, and especially to the midnight service that evening.

As Hamish looked out of the cottage window, the evening skies turned from soft pink to coral to dark blue. Christmas Day was just a twinkling star away. Soft snow was tumbling like icing sugar sieved over Dorma's Christmas pies to be blown by the North wind into deep meringue peaks. All over the city yellow and orange lights shone from cottage windows, and the Christmas trees placed in the windows had lights which sparked on and off in gay colours, making jewelled reflections in the snow crystals.

"The Christmas service will be wonderful this year. I'm so looking forward to it. We'll all have such a good time " said Hamish as he joined Dorma and Aunt Maude in the sitting room.

"Hamish, really!" snorted Aunt Maude. "Dorma and I will not be going to the midnight service. For pity's sake can't you remember what is supposed to be happening tomorrow?" Another one of Aunt Maude's trick questions, Hamish thought. Everybody knows it's Christmas Day'; but he was puzzled all the same. "Dorma, you never miss the Christmas Service!" pleaded Hamish.

"I am afraid that this year, I must, Hamish dear", said Dorma kindly and one look from Aunt Maude was enough to stop any further protests from Hamish.

The cathedral bells began to ring out over the silent city, calling all who wished to attend

to come to the midnight service. Hamish was ready in his anorak and boots with his bagpipes proudly stored in their leather bag under his arm, as he kissed Dorma on the cheek and stepped out alone into the midnight winter scene.

"Play well, Hamish, I will be thinking of you," said Dorma as she blew a soft kiss from her hand in his direction and gently closed the door.

Hamish made his lonely way though the Kirk yard under a deep velvet-blue sky, lit by a crescent moon. The icy wind, which had travelled from the arctic especially for the occasion, but had not been invited to the service, whined and whirled spitefully around him. Crisp snow crunched under his boots and a cold tingle on his whiskers told him it had started to snow again.

When Hamish reached the cathedral a happy chatter of mice was waiting to greet him. Folk were gathering from all corners of the old city – some came on sledges, some on foot.

Some even had skis. Young mice, whom on this special night had been allowed to stay up, gathered mittens of snow and hurled snowballs at each other outside the door. The minister stood near a tall green pine tree, which was garlanded with hundreds of tiny twinkling lights glistening -like early morning frost. With a smile he greeted all who entered. Each mouse was handed a long white candle to carry into the service which when lit illuminated their happy Christmas faces in a pool of pale yellow light. Coloured lights twinkled in nooks and crannies of the old stone walls, splashing them with yellow, then green, then red Christmas light.

Soon it was time for Hamish to play his part in the service. He stood up and walked from his pew to the front of the cathedral. Scores of little mice eyes followed him as he strode proudly before the silk-covered altar. He took his bagpipes from their bag, straightened his kilt, inflated the bag and took the chanters into his hands.

There can be no more beautiful sound than the echoing melody of the bagpipes played by a master - and Hamish McMoosie could truly play the bagpipes. The congregation fell quiet, whispers died

away, as the haunting sound of "Silent Night" filled the air. It seemed that the very walls of the ancient cathedral stood in awe at the sound. Folk passing by outside were heard to remark that the wind played strange tricks tonight – it sounded like Angel's music.

Hamish had much to tell Dorma when he reached home. He wanted to tell her how well the service had gone, pass on all the good wishes from the mice folk and especially about his playing the bagpipes and how proud he had been. He hoped that she had not yet gone to bed, "Dorma", he called as he opened the door, "Dorma?"

"In here, Hamish, with Aunt Maude" called Dorma from their bedroom down the hall.

'Whatever is going on?'" thought Hamish, striding down the hall to their bedroom. He stepped into the softly lit bedroom. What a sight caught his eyes!

A smiling Dorma was sitting up in bed, and snuggled beside her, wearing fluffy, yellow, Angora wool bootees were one, two, three baby mice, all fast asleep. "Our own wee baby mice" smiled Dorma.

"Oh my!" said Hamish, " I didn't know...How? When? What a Christmas present! To think I thought you were knitting covers for my golf clubs!"

Hamish, in a moment of uncontrolled happiness even gave Aunt Maude a kiss, and in the corner of Aunt Maude's eye a tear of joy glistened.

Outside, high in the dark, clear night sky over the tiny cottage hidden under the old house, a single star shone brightly.

The  End

NEW EXCITING ADVENTURES TO COME